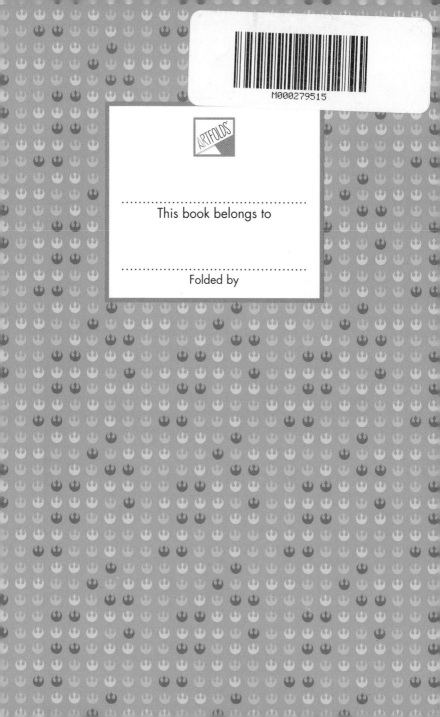

ARTFOLDS

....
This book belongs to

....
Folded by

ARTFOLDS®

COLOR EDITIONS NO. 6

YODA AND THE FORCE

The Way of the Jedi

Studio Fun
White Plains, New York • Montréal, Québec • Bath, United Kingdom

ArtFolds
Color Editions No. 6
Yoda and the Force
© & TM 2015 LUCASFILM LTD.

ArtFolds is a patent-pending process.

ArtFolds is a registered trademark and Studio Fun Books is a trademark of
Studio Fun International, Inc., a subsidiary of The Reader's Digest Association, Inc.

ISBN 978-0-7944-3492-2

To learn more about ArtFolds, visit www.artfolds.com.

Customized and/or prefolded ArtFolds are available. To explore options and
pricing, email specialorder@artfolds.com.

To discover the wide range of products available from Studio Fun International,
visit www.studiofun.com.

Address any comments about ArtFolds to:
Publisher
Studio Fun Books
44 South Broadway, 7th floor
White Plains, NY 10601

Or send an email to publisher@artfolds.com.

Printed in China
Conforms to ASTM F963

10 9 8 7 6 5 4 3 2 1   LPP/05/15

About ArtFolds

THE BOOK YOU HOLD in your hands is more than just a book. It's an ArtFolds®! Inside are simple instructions that will show you how to fold the pages to transform this book into a beautiful sculpture. No special skill is required; all you'll do is carefully fold the corners of marked book pages, based on the folding lines provided. When complete, you'll have created a long-lasting work of art. It's fun and easy, and can be completed in just one evening!

To add to the experience, each ArtFolds contains compelling reading content. In this edition, you'll enjoy reading quotations from *Star Wars* characters—especially Yoda—sharing their Jedi knowledge.

Each ArtFolds edition is designed by an established, professional book sculptor whose works are routinely displayed and sold in art galleries, museum shops, and online crafts and art stores. ArtFolds celebrates this community of artists and encourages you to support this expanding art form by seeking out their work and sharing their unique designs and creations with others.

To learn more about ArtFolds, visit www.artfolds.com. There you'll find details of all ArtFolds® editions, instructional videos, and much more.

Instructions

Creating your ArtFolds Color Editions book sculpture is easy! Just follow these simple instructions and guidelines:

1. Always fold right-hand pages.

2. Always fold toward you.

3. All folding pages require two folds: the top corner will fold down, and the bottom corner will fold up.

4. Grasp the top right corner of the page, and fold until the side of the page aligns exactly with the TOP of the horizontal color bar.

5. Grasp the bottom right corner of the page, and fold upward until the side of the page aligns exactly with the BOTTOM of the horizontal color bar.

6. Carefully run your finger across the folds to make sure they are straight, crisp, and accurate.

7. Continue on to the next page and repeat until your ArtFolds book sculpture is complete!

Extra advice

- We recommend washing and then thoroughly drying your hands prior to folding.

- Some folders prefer using a tool to help make fold lines straight and sharp. Bone folders, metal rulers, popsicle sticks, or any other firm, straight tool will work.

- Some folders prefer to rotate their book sideways to make folding easier.

- Remember: The more accurate you are with each fold, the more accurate your completed book sculpture will be!

- Right after the book has been folded, it may fan out broadly. To compress the sculpture, close it and wrap it in a couple of rubber bands for a day or two.

Folding begins right after the full-page portrait of Yoda!

For more folding instructions and videos, visit www.artfolds.com.

YODA AND THE FORCE

The Way of the Jedi

BEINGS FROM ALL OVER THE GALAXY WERE BROUGHT TO CORUSCANT TO TRAIN TO BECOME JEDI KNIGHTS. Those Jedi hopefuls came across a diminutive but intimidating figure named Yoda. Jedi Master and member of the Jedi Council, Yoda spent hundreds of years training the most dedicated Jedi in the ways of the Force. Such famous Jedi as Obi-Wan Kenobi and Qui-Gon Jinn were fortunate enough to have called Yoda their Master.

For a thousand years, the Jedi Order had maintained peace and justice in the Republic, keeping it free from the threat of the deadly Sith, enemies of the Jedi and adherents to the dark side of the Force. However, the galaxy was soon in the throes of a battle of light against dark, the Jedi versus the unseen forces of a Sith Lord. The Republic eventually fell and the Jedi Order was extinguished, but Master Yoda survived to pass on what he had learned and to bring hope back to the galaxy.

Yoda and the Force brings together words of knowledge, struggle, excitement, and even fear from all six of the epic *Star Wars* films, featuring quotations from Master Yoda as well as other Jedi such as Qui-Gon Jinn, Obi-Wan Kenobi, Mace Windu, and Anakin Skywalker. Also featured are the sworn enemies of the Jedi, Darth Sidious, Darth Maul, Count Dooku, and Darth Vader, as the battle to bring balance to the Force rages from the center of the galaxy to the dusty, desert planets of the Outer Rim.

**Master Yoda says I should be
mindful of the future.**

– Obi-Wan Kenobi

Don't center on your anxieties, Obi-Wan. Keep your concentration here and now where it belongs.

– Qui-Gon Jinn

Be mindful of the living Force.

– Qui-Gon Jinn

There's always a bigger fish.

– Qui-Gon Jinn

I sense a disturbance in the Force.

– Qui-Gon Jinn

**Concentrate on the moment.
Feel, don't think.
Trust your instincts.**

– Qui-Gon Jinn

Fear is the path to the dark side.

– Yoda

Fear leads to anger. Anger leads to hate. Hate leads to suffering.

– Yoda

Hard to see, the dark side is.

– Yoda

Yoda: **Always two there are...no more, no less. A master and an apprentice.**

Mace Windu: **But which one was destroyed? The master or the apprentice?**

START
FOLDING
HERE

**Qui-Gon's defiance I sense in you.
Need that you do not.**

– Yoda

You must realize there aren't enough Jedi to protect the Republic. We're keepers of the peace, not soldiers.

– Mace Windu

The dark side clouds everything. Impossible to see, the future is.

– Yoda

Dreams pass in time.

– Obi-Wan Kenobi

You want to go home and rethink your life.

– Obi-Wan Kenobi

If you spent as much time practicing your saber techniques as you do your wit, you would rival Master Yoda as a swordsman.

– Obi-Wan Kenobi

Sometimes we must let go of our pride and do what is requested of us.

– Anakin Skywalker

Obi-Wan is a great mentor. As wise as Master Yoda and as powerful as Master Windu. I am truly thankful to be his apprentice.

– Anakin Skywalker

Reach out. Sense the Force around you.

– Yoda

Attachment is forbidden. Possession is forbidden. Compassion, which I would define as unconditional love, is central to a Jedi's life. So you might say that we are encouraged to love.

– Anakin Skywalker

Use your feelings you must.

– Yoda

Gravity's silhouette remains, but the star and all its planets, disappeared they have.

– Yoda

Truly wonderful the mind of a child is.

– Yoda

**Go to the center of gravity's pull
and find your planet you will.**

– Yoda

**Do not assume anything, Obi-Wan.
Clear your mind must be if you are to discover
the real villains behind this plot.**

– Yoda

**Powerful you have become, Dooku.
The dark side I sense in you.**

– Yoda

Much to learn you still have.

– Yoda

It is obvious that this contest cannot be decided by our knowledge of the Force, but by our skills with a lightsaber.

– Count Dooku

Joined the dark side Dooku has. Lies, deceit, creating mistrust are his ways now.

– Yoda

**The shroud of the dark side has fallen.
Begun the Clone War has.**

– Yoda

**I sense great fear in you, Skywalker.
You have fate, you have anger,
but you don't use them.**

– Count Dooku

**Attachment leads to jealousy.
The shadow of greed, that is.**

– Yoda

**Rejoice for those around you
who transform into the Force.
Mourn them do not. Miss them do not.**

– Yoda

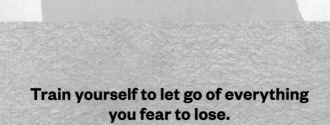

Train yourself to let go of everything you fear to lose.

– Yoda

I can feel your anger. It gives you focus.

– Chancellor Palpatine

If one is to understand the great mystery, one must study all its aspects, not just the narrow, dogmatic view of the Jedi. If you wish to become a complete and wise leader, you must embrace a larger view of the Force.

– Chancellor Palpatine

In a dark place we find ourselves.
A little more knowledge might light our way.

– Yoda

Only a Sith Lord deals in absolutes.

– Obi-Wan Kenobi

**At an end your rule is and
not short enough it was, I must say.**
– Yoda

**I have waited a long time for this moment,
my little green friend.**

– Emperor Palpatine

Faith in your new apprentice, misplaced may be. As is your faith in the dark side of the Force.

– Yoda

Into exile I must go. Failed I have.

– Yoda

Until the time is right, disappear we will.

– Yoda

For a thousand generations the Jedi Knights were the guardians of peace and justice in the Republic. Before the dark times. Before the Empire.

– Obi-Wan Kenobi

**The Force is what gives a Jedi his power.
It's an energy field created by all living things.
It surrounds us and penetrates us.
It binds the galaxy together.**

– Obi-Wan Kenobi

The Force can have a strong influence on the weak-minded.

– Obi-Wan Kenobi

**Remember, a Jedi can feel
the Force flowing through him.**

– Obi-Wan Kenobi

Your eyes can deceive you. Don't trust them.

– Obi-Wan Kenobi

Stretch out with your feelings.

– Obi-Wan Kenobi

**Who's the more foolish...
the fool or the fool who follows him?**

– Obi-Wan Kenobi

The Force will be with you...always.

– Obi-Wan Kenobi

Trust your feelings.

– Obi-Wan Kenobi

**Luke, you will go to the Dagobah system.
There you will learn from Yoda,
the Jedi Master who instructed me.**

– Obi-Wan Kenobi

**Now all I've got to do is find this Yoda...
if he even exists. It's really a strange place
to find a Jedi Master.**

– Luke Skywalker

Wars not make one great.

– Yoda

Patience!
For the Jedi it is time to eat as well.

– Yoda

Yoda: **Why wish you become Jedi, hmm?**
Luke: **Mostly because of my father, I guess.**
Yoda: **Ah, father. Powerful Jedi was he.**

Yoda:
Hmmm. Much anger in him, like his father.

Obi-Wan Kenobi:
Was I any different when you taught me?

For eight hundred years have I trained Jedi.

– Yoda

**My own counsel I will keep on
who is to be trained!**

– Yoda

A Jedi must have the deepest commitment, the most serious mind.

– Yoda

**This one, a long time have I watched.
All his life has he looked away to the future, to
the horizon. Never his mind on where he was.
What he was doing.**

– Yoda

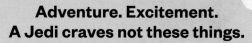

**Adventure. Excitement.
A Jedi craves not these things.**

– Yoda

Luke: **I'm not afraid.**

Yoda: **You will be. You will be.**

A Jedi's strength flows from the Force.

– Yoda

**But beware of the dark side.
Anger...fear...aggression.
The dark side of the Force are they.
Easily they flow, quick to join you in a fight.**

– Yoda

If once you start down the dark path, forever will it dominate your destiny, consume you it will.

– Yoda

Luke: **Is the dark side stronger?**

Yoda: **No...no...no. Quicker, easier, more seductive.**

Luke:
But how am I to know the good from the bad?

Yoda:
**You will know. When you are calm, at peace.
Passive.**

A Jedi uses the Force for knowledge and defense, never for attack.

– Yoda

There is no why.

– Yoda

Clear your mind of questions.

– Yoda

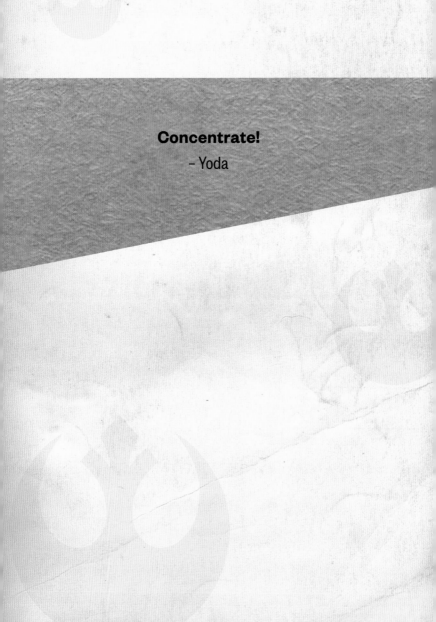

Concentrate!
– Yoda

Always with you what cannot be done.

– Yoda

You must unlearn what you have learned.

– Yoda

Try not. Do. Or do not. There is no try.

– Yoda

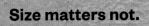

Size matters not.

– Yoda

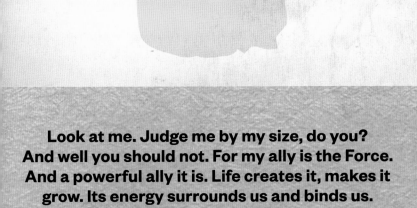

Look at me. Judge me by my size, do you? And well you should not. For my ally is the Force. And a powerful ally it is. Life creates it, makes it grow. Its energy surrounds us and binds us.

– Yoda

Luminous beings are we...not this crude matter.

– Yoda

You must feel the Force around you.

– Yoda

Luke: **I don't believe it!**

Yoda: **That is why you fail.**

Through the Force, things you will see. Other places. The future...the past. Old friends long gone.

– Yoda

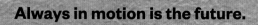

Always in motion is the future.

– Yoda

**Only a fully trained Jedi Knight
with the Force as his ally will conquer
Vader and his Emperor.**

– Yoda

If you end your training now, if you choose the quick and easy path, as Vader did, you will become an agent of evil.

– Yoda

Mind what you have learned. Save you it can!

– Yoda

Don't give in to hate—that leads to the dark side.

– Obi-Wan Kenobi

**Obi-Wan has taught you well.
You have controlled your fear.
Now release your anger.**

– Darth Vader

**With our combined strength,
we can end this destructive conflict
and bring order to the galaxy!**

– Darth Vader

When nine hundred years old you reach, look as good you will not!

– Yoda

**Soon I will rest. Yes, forever sleep.
Earned it, I have.**

– Yoda

Luke:
I've come back to complete the training.

Yoda:
No more training do you require. Already know you that which you need.

**Remember, a Jedi's strength
flows from the Force.**

– Yoda

But beware. Anger, fear, aggression. The dark side of the Force are they.

– Yoda

**Once you start down the dark path,
forever will it dominate your destiny.**

– Yoda

**Luke, when gone am I...the last
of the Jedi will you be.**

– Yoda

**Luke, the Force runs strong in your family.
Pass on what you have learned.**

– Yoda

Luke, there is another Skywalker.

– Yoda

**Your father was seduced by
the dark side of the Force. He ceased
to be Anakin Skywalker and became
Darth Vader. When that happened,
the good man who was your father
was destroyed.**

– Obi-Wan Kenobi

Luke, you're going to find that many of the truths we cling to depend greatly on our own point of view.

– Obi-Wan Kenobi

**Your insight serves you well.
Bury your feelings deep down, Luke.
They do you credit. But they could be made
to serve the Emperor.**

– Obi-Wan Kenobi

**The Force is strong in my family.
My father has it...I have it...and my sister has it.**

– Luke Skywalker

There is good in him. I've felt it. He won't turn me over to the Emperor. I can save him. I can turn him back to the good side. I have to try.

– Luke Skywalker

**You don't know the power of the dark side.
I must obey my Master.**

– Darth Vader

**I feel the conflict within you.
Let go of your hate.**

– Luke Skywalker

**I'll never turn to the dark side.
You've failed, your highness. I am a Jedi,
like my father before me.**

– Luke Skywalker

Luke:
I'll not leave you here. I've got to save you.

Anakin:
**You already have, Luke. You were right.
You were right about me. Tell your sister...
you were right.**

Yoda will always be with you.

– Obi-Wan Kenobi

About the Designer

The sculpture design in this edition was created exclusively for ArtFolds by **Luciana Frigerio**. Based in Vermont, Luciana has been making photographs, objects, book sculptures, and artistic mischief for over 30 years. Her work has been exhibited in galleries and museums around the world. Luciana's artwork can be found at: www.lucianafrigerio.com, and her unique, customized book sculptures can be found in her shop on the online crafts market Etsy at: www.etsy.com/shop/LucianaFrigerio.

The ArtFolds Portfolio

Color Editions

These smaller ArtFolds editions use a range of colors printed on each page to make each sculpture a multi-colored work of art. Titles now or soon available include:

Edition 1: Heart
Edition 2: Mickey Mouse
Edition 3: Christmas Tree
Edition 4: MOM
Edition 5: Flower
Edition 6: Yoda

Classic Editions

These larger ArtFolds editions include the full text of a classic book; when folded, book text appears along the edges, creating a piece of art that celebrates the dignity and beauty of a printed book. Titles now or soon available include:

Edition 1: LOVE
Edition 2: Snowflake
Edition 3: JOY
Edition 4: READ
Edition 5: Sun
Edition 6: Darth Vader

To see the full range of ArtFolds editions, visit www.artfolds.com.

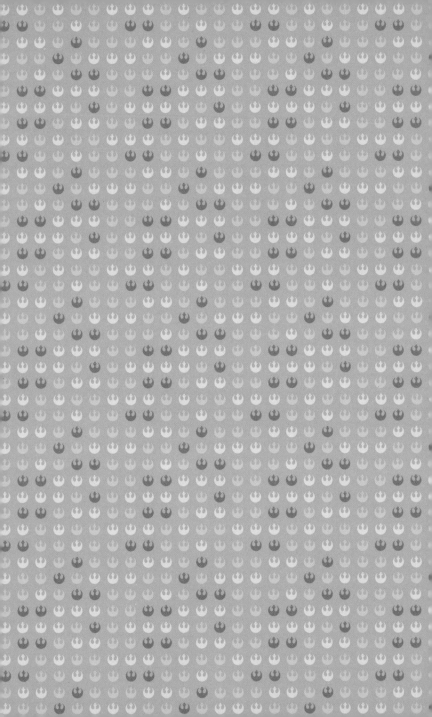